Fondly dedicated to our childlike alter
egos...Ishey, Elizabeth, Joey, Buckey,
Clifford and Uncle Joey (my husband),
who made it all possible.

M.M.

The UGLY SNOWFLAKE

Written and Sung by
Micki McHay

Illustrated by
Frank Fiorello

First Edition
10 9 8 7 6 5 4 3 2 1

ISBN: 0-9786826-0-2

Summary: With the help of a special angel, the Ugly Snowflake discovers her true beauty.

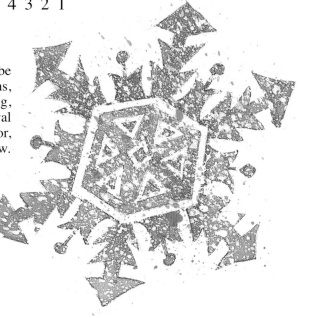

Many years ago on a wonderful Christmas night, all the land was white with snow and the snowflakes were dancing from the sky.

They sparkled and glistened over the hills
and each of their colors was so magnificent, it was
as though God had taken every color of the rainbow
and intertwined it with silvery gold.

And as they danced, it was a splendid sight and for a moment, the world stood still as they danced the Dance of the Snowflakes.

But off in the distance there was one poor little, lonely snowflake, so plain, she had no dazzle. Her coat was black and covered with branches and soot, from landing in trees and dirty old chimneys.

She would stand in the background looking at all of the lovely snowflakes and so long to be a part of their beautiful, beautiful dance.

But the other snowflakes would laugh at her and poke fun at her and tell her that she was ugly and plain.

You're
ugly!

You're
plain!

You're
a real
flake!

And the poor ugly snowflake would cry because she was so clumsy and she knew it, and she would sing this sad, sad song.

Why couldn't I have been a pretty little snowflake
falling from the sky, falling from the sky.
And why couldn't I have been beautiful and fine.
I'd be so proud I would absolutely shine...

And why couldn't I have been a pretty little snowflake,
dainty as a thrush and never turn to slush.
Oh, why...why...why.

ut hark, far off in the distance stood a beautiful lady with long blonde hair and a shimmering gown. It was the Angel of Christmas.

$\mathcal{S}$he came up to the ugly snowflake
and asked her what was wrong.

And the snowflake told
her that none of the
other snowflakes wanted
to be a part of her,
and that she was alone
and she really had no one.

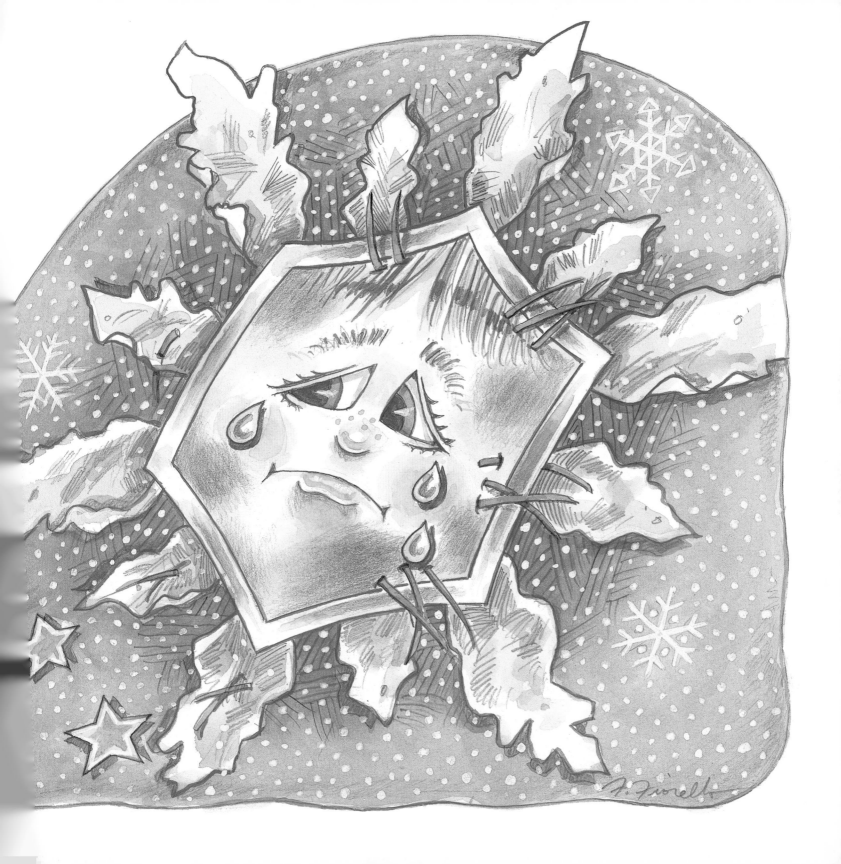

And the Angel of Christmas looked at her and smiled, for she already knew what the ugly snowflake was going through and this is what she said...

Everybody wants to be original,
everybody wants to be a shining star.
If you really want to be special,
you have to stay who you are...

And when the others
start poking fun at you,
you have to stand tall and
know that you are you.

Suddenly the ugly snowflake realized what the Angel of Christmas meant, and at that very moment, something began happening to her...it was as if she was being reborn. She felt a freedom she had never known before. She was no longer clumsy and awkward... she was SPECTACULAR!

And when the other snowflakes saw this, they stood in awe of her...

Ah, look, she's glistening!

They came up to her and not a word was spoken. They just stood there and glowed with love.

And it truly was a wonderful Christmas, and once again, the world stood still as the Angel of Christmas waved her wand and the lights of Heaven shone down upon them as they danced the Dance of the Snowflakes.

There's a little snowflake

in all of us!